nickelodeon

# SPRING is EVERYWHERE!

A Random House PICTUREBACK® Book

Random House New York

 Published in the United States by Random House Children's Books, a division of Penguin Random House LLC, 1745 Broadway, New York, NY 10019, and in Canada by Penguin Random House Canada Limited, Toronto. These stories were originally published separately in different form by Random House as *The Pups Save the Bunnies* in 2016, *Zeg and the Egg* in 2016, *Bug Parade!* in 2014, and *Marshall to the Rescue!* in 2016.

randomhousekids.com
ISBN 978-1-524-70067-6
MANUFACTURED IN CHINA
10 9

# CONTENTS

# THE PUPS SAVE THE BUNNIES

Based on the teleplay "Pup Saves the Bunnies" by Ursula Ziegler-Sullivan
Illustrated by MJ Illustrations

It was a sunny day, and Mr. Porter was visiting Farmer Yumi to get some carrots for his market. But there was a problem. . . . The carrots were disappearing into the dirt!

"These carrots are growing backward!" Mr. Porter exclaimed.

But Farmer Yumi knew what was really happening—bunnies were eating her carrots.

This was a job for the PAW Patrol!

Ryder called the PAW Patrol to the Lookout and told them about the bunnies.

"We need to move the bunnies to a field where they'll be safe and won't eat Farmer Yumi's carrots. Rubble, I'll need your shovel so we can find the bunnies' tunnels."

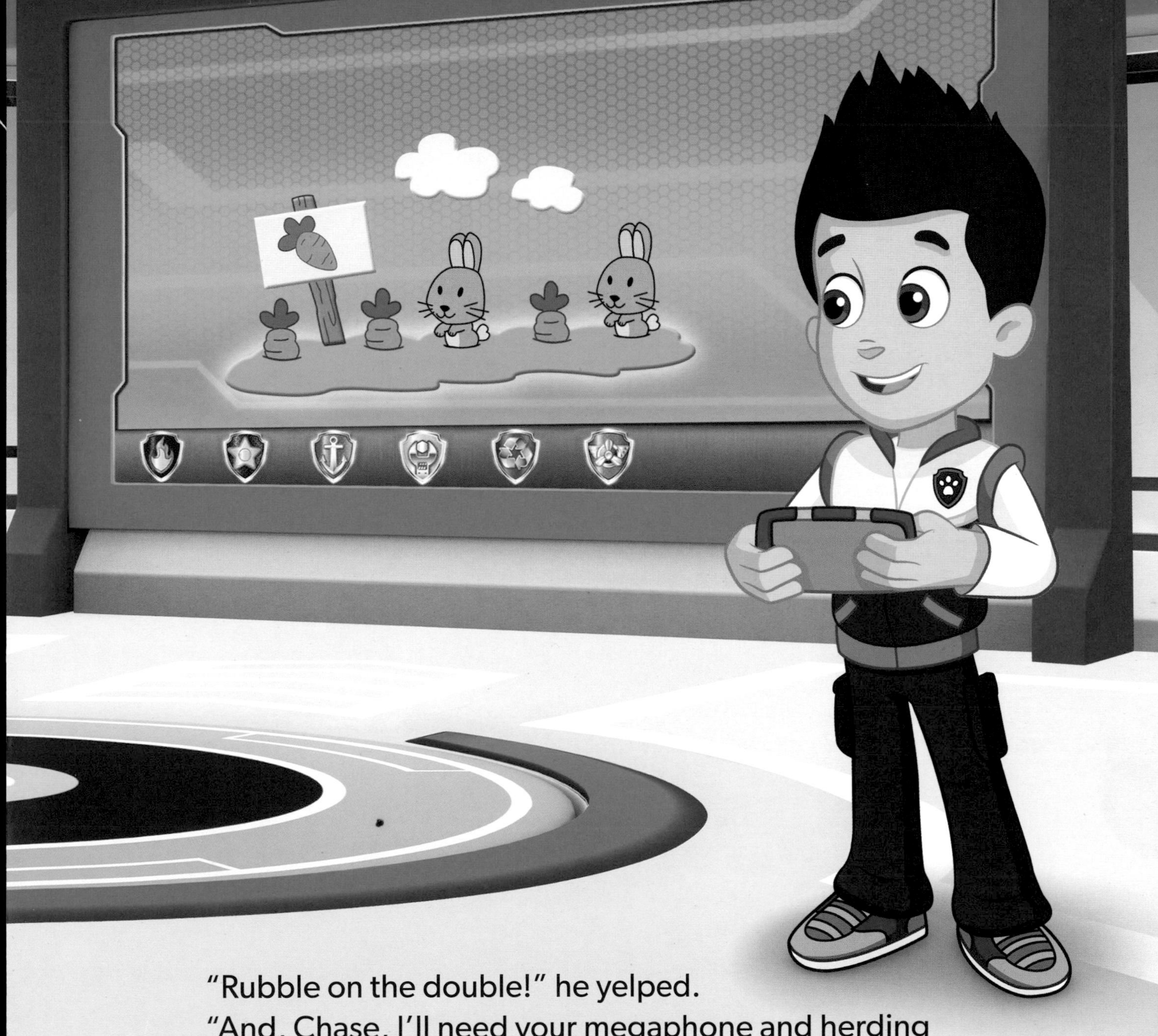

"Rubble on the double!" he yelped.

"And, Chase, I'll need your megaphone and herding skills to round up the bunnies," Ryder continued.

"Chase is on the case!" the police pup exclaimed.

Ryder, Rubble, and Chase raced to Farmer Yumi's Farm.

"Let's dig in!" Rubble said, and he started digging for the bunny tunnels. "I think I found something!" he shouted a few moments later. "In fact, I found *two* somethings!"

Ryder needed a way to carry the two bunnies from the farm. He called Rocky and Skye on his PupPad. "Rocky, can you get some old kennel cages so Skye can fly them here?"

"Don't lose it—reuse it!" Rocky said.

"And I'll be there in two shakes of a bunny's tail," Skye added.

Skye arrived with the kennel cages, and Chase started herding the bunnies into them.

"Attention, all bunnies!" Chase announced through his megaphone. "We brought cages with nice, soft beds to take you to your new homes."

"And inside each cage," Skye said, "is a crunchy treat."

The bunnies hopped into the cages, and Skye lifted off in her copter to take them to their new field.

But the busy day wasn't over yet! When Mr. Porter returned to his market, he found some furry-tailed surprises in the box of vegetables he'd brought from the farm.

This was another job for the PAW Patrol!

The team sped to Mr. Porter's market.

"I need some of your delicious carrot cake, Mr. Porter," Ryder said. He had a plan for how to collect the bunnies.

Ryder set the cake on the ground, and all the bunnies bounded over to it. "Now we need your net, Chase!"

Chase launched his net over the bunnies, and Ryder carefully scooped them up.

Skye carried the last of the bunnies to their new home in the faraway field. As soon as Ryder opened the kennel cages, the little bunnies bounced into the grass and began to happily munch on flowers.

"Bye-bye, bunnies," Skye said. "I'm going to miss you."

When Skye returned to the Lookout, she realized she wasn't alone—a bunny had stowed away with her! "Can we keep her?"

"We can handle *one* bunny," Ryder said.

"Ryder, you're the best," Skye cheered as the pups welcomed their new furry friend.

By Mary Tillworth

Illustrated by Niki Foley

Blaze and AJ loved to race! But they also liked to spend time with their friend Zeg.

"We're playing Zeg's favorite game. It's called Smash!" said Blaze.

"Smash! Smash!" yelled Zeg and Blaze as they smashed through rocks and bashed through boulders.

"Big yellow rock with purple spots," said Zeg. "Zeg never see rock like this before."

It was a dinosaur egg! Blaze
and Zeg had to return it to its nest.

The monster trucks sped through a narrow canyon—and came upon a giant coconut!

"Lug nuts!" Blaze exclaimed. "There's no way to go around it."

The coconut was even too big for Zeg to smash. But then Blaze had an idea—a wedge!

"A wedge is a simple machine you can use to split stuff," he said.

He put the pointy part of the wedge against the coconut, then banged on the flat side. The coconut started to crack.

Zeg gave the wedge a really good bash and the whole coconut fell apart.

"Zeg like wedge!" the dinosaur truck exclaimed as he drove through the canyon.

When Blaze and Zeg zoomed out of the canyon, they saw something amazing. There was a giant volcano, and lava was oozing down its sides!

"Zeg have to protect egg!" growled the dinosaur truck.

Blaze knew that water would stop the lava. He used his wedge to crack open a giant water barrel. Water splashed across the ground and cooled the lava. Blaze, his friends, and the egg were all safe!

Zeg took good care of the egg. He used a blanket to keep it warm.

"Here, egg. Zeg make blanket for you. Nice and cozy," he said.

But Crusher grabbed the blanket, and the egg flew way up in the air! It landed on a mountaintop.

"I made a terrible mistake!" said Crusher. "Someone's got to rescue that egg!"

Blaze and Zeg zoomed up the rocky cliff. They dodged boulders and smashed through rocks until they reached the top—and saved the egg!

The two Monster Machines raced back through the jungle and returned the egg to its nest. The moment they got it home, something amazing happened. It hatched!

"You not egg anymore. You baby dinosaur . . . and you so cute," said Zeg. Blaze and AJ smiled.

The baby dinosaur wanted to thank Zeg and his friends. He flew into the air and kissed each of them on the hood.

Hooray for Blaze and the Monster Machines!

Bubble Guppies™

# Bug Parade!

By Krista Pohlmeyer

Based on the teleplay "Bring on the Bugs!" by Jonny Belt, Bob Mittenthal, Michael Rubiner, Robert Scull, and Clark Stubbs

Illustrated by Harry Moore

Molly and Gil were on their way to school.
"Oh, look!" Molly said. "It's a spiderweb!"
"I wonder where the spider is," Gil said.

Soon a spider crawled out onto the web.
"There he is!" Gil said. "I'll name him Charlie."

"I bet he's trying to catch his breakfast," said Gil.

"Breakfast? What do you mean?" Molly asked.

"When they're finished building their webs, spiders wait for flies to get caught in them. Then . . . they eat them!"

"Well, we can come back later and see if he's caught anything," Molly said. "Come on, Gil."

"Okay. Bye, Charlie!" Gil said.

"Good morning, Mr. Grouper!" Molly and Gil said when they got to school.

"Boy, have I got a treat for you kids today!" Mr. Grouper said.

"What is it?" the class asked.

"We're going to be in a bug parade," Mr. Grouper said. "Grab some costumes!"

"The bug parade is about to begin!" Deema said, pretending to be a reporter. "There are marching ants, flying balloons, and lots of floats!"

Charlie the spider was watching from his brand-new web.

Nonny marched in the Marching Ants Marching Band.

He danced like he had ants in his pants. But the ants were in the band!

Oona the ladybug rode on a float covered in flowers. Even Bubble Puppy was dressed up—as a grasshopper! What a *hoppy* puppy!

Goby the dragonfly flew all around the parade. He was flying so fast, he was passing everyone!

The class had seen a horsefly, a housefly, and even a dragonfly . . . but they'd never seen a Bubble Guppy fly!

Molly and Gil were "bugging out" on the spider float, especially when they discovered that spiders aren't insects—they're arachnids!

Just then, the wind picked up. Some of the big bug balloons were flying away! A crab tried as hard as he could to hold on to his fly balloon!

It was no use. The fly balloon was flying away!

The fly balloon was headed right for Charlie's spiderweb.

Molly and Gil sprang into action! They used ropes to make a giant spiderweb between the balloon and Charlie's web.

The spiderweb caught the fly balloon just in time. Charlie and his web were safe! *Swim*-sational!

The Guppies rushed to Charlie's web.

"Are you okay?" Molly asked him.

Charlie quickly moved around his web to make a heart out of silk for his friends!

"Aww, you're welcome, Charlie!" Gil said.

The bug parade was saved!

# Marshall to the Rescue!

Based on the episode "Pup Pup Goose" by Ursula Ziegler-Sullivan

Illustrated by MJ Illustrations

It was an exciting day at the Lookout. A flock of geese was flying south for the winter, and the birds were going to stop at the Lookout for a rest. To welcome them, Rocky, Marshall, and Chase built a big nest, and Rubble used his shovel to fill it with yummy bread.

The geese landed and immediately started pecking at the bread. One tired goose happily settled into the nest to relax.

"He likes your nest," Ryder said, patting Rocky.

But a baby goose wandered away from the rest of the flock. He waddled into a blue bucket—and rolled down a hill!

"I'll get him!" Marshall announced, racing after the bucket. As he ran down the hill, his feet got tangled. Marshall *and* the goose ended up bouncing down the hill!

When they reached the bottom, they were both a little dizzy.

"Are you okay, fuzzy little guy?" Marshall asked.

*"Cheep! Cheep!"* the goose replied with a nod.

"Hey!" Marshall exclaimed. "Fuzzy is a great name for you!"

Marshall took Fuzzy back to the Lookout, where he introduced him to the rest of the PAW Patrol. The little goose liked all the pups, but Marshall was definitely his favorite.

Skye chuckled. "Marshall, it looks like you have a new BGFF—Best Goose Friend Forever!"

For the rest of the day, the two friends did everything together. When Marshall tripped over his dog bowl, so did Fuzzy.

When Marshall washed his fire truck, Fuzzy polished the window with his feathers . . .

. . . until Marshall accidentally "washed" him with his hose!
"Sorry, Fuzzy," said Marshall.

When it was time for bed, the two friends snuggled together under the stars.

Just before dawn, Fuzzy woke up. He was hungry, so he wandered off, looking for food.

Marshall woke up later and couldn't find the little goose. He was worried, so he went to Ryder.

Ryder called the PAW Patrol to the Lookout.

"Our geese friends have to fly south for the winter," he explained. "If we don't find Fuzzy fast, they'll have to leave without him!"

Outside the Lookout, Chase called to the lost goose. Marshall sniffed the ground in search of clues. He found one of Fuzzy's feathers! Ryder picked it up, and Chase took a whiff.

*"ACHOO!"* Chase sneezed. "Sorry—I'm a little allergic to feathers." He took a few more sniffs, sneezed, and announced, "He went this way!"

Ryder, Chase, and Marshall jumped into their vehicles and followed Fuzzy's trail into Adventure Bay.

The team spotted Fuzzy on the roof of the train station. He had a piece of bread, and some seagulls were trying to take it. He couldn't fly away because a plastic soda-can ring was wrapped around his wing.

"Marshall, quick!" Ryder exclaimed. "Use your ladder to help get Fuzzy down!"

Marshall extended the ladder on his fire truck, which scared away the seagulls. As he started to climb up, Fuzzy tried to run to him—and fell! Marshall quickly held out his fire helmet and caught the little goose.

"Sweet catch, Marshall!" Ryder cheered.

Back on the ground, Ryder carefully removed the plastic ring from Fuzzy. The little bird was free. He could fly again!

The PAW Patrol raced back to the Lookout. They had to get there before Fuzzy's flock flew away.

But they were too late—the geese had just left! Fuzzy would have to flap fast to catch up to them.

Fuzzy didn't want to go, and Marshall didn't want him to leave, either.

"A little gosling belongs with his family," Ryder said.

Marshall agreed, and Ryder quickly came up with a plan to return Fuzzy to his flock.

"Let's take to the sky!" Skye exclaimed as her helicopter zoomed into the air, pulling Marshall along in a harness.

"Come on, Fuzzy!" Marshall shouted. "Time to fly with me! Flap! Flap!"

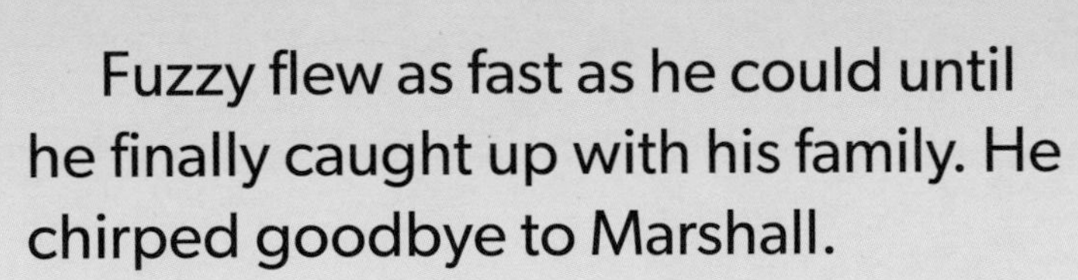

Fuzzy flew as fast as he could until he finally caught up with his family. He chirped goodbye to Marshall.

"Goodbye, Fuzzy," Marshall called with a teary sniffle. "Have a safe flight, you silly goose!"

Back at the Lookout, the pups played jump rope.

"You guys did an awesome job today," Ryder said.

Marshall missed Fuzzy, but he knew his little friend would visit whenever his family flew overhead. Until then, he had his *paw*some pup pals to keep him company!